WILEY & GRAMPA'S CREATURE FEATURES

SUPER SOCCER FREAK SHOW

WRITTEN AND
ILLUSTRATED BY

KIRK SCROGGS

A TAIL WITH BITE!

13

LITTLE, BRO
New York ~ Bosto

In memory of Dan Hooker, super agent and believer in Grampa

———————

Special thanks to:
Ashley & Carolyn Grayson, Suppasak Viboonlarp, Mark
Mayes, Jim Jeong, Joe Kocian, Hiland Hall, Steve Deline, Jackie
Greed, the mezz crew-Woo Woo!

Andrea, Sangeeta, Saho, Alison, Elizabeth, Tina
and the Little, Brown crew-hooray!

And a super deep-dish thanks with extra cheese to Diane and Corey
Scroggs and Harold and Betty Aulds.

Little, Brown and Company

Hachette Book Group USA
1271 Avenue of the Americas, New York, NY 10020
Visit our Web site at www.lb-kids.com

First Edition: January 2007

Library of Congress Cataloging-in-Publication Data

Scroggs, Kirk.
  Super Soccer Freak Show / written and illustrated by Kirk Scroggs.—1st ed.
    p. cm.—(Wiley & Grampa's creature features ; #4)
  Summary: When Grampa is bitten by a rival soccer team's mascot and turns into a were-yote,
members of the Ladies' Quilting League offer to destroy him, but Hans Lotion has a solution
that could be less deadly.
  ISBN-13: 978-0-316-05946-6 (hardcover) / ISBN-10: 0-316-05946-3 (hardcover)
  ISBN-13: 978-0-316-05947-3 (pbk.) / ISBN-10: 0-316-05947-1 (pbk.)
  [1. Grandparents—Fiction. 2. Werewolves—Fiction. 3. Soccer—Fiction. 4. Humorous stories.]
I. Title. II. Series: Scroggs, Kirk. Wiley & Grampa's creature features ; #4.
PZ7.S436726How 2007
[Fic]—dc22   2005057779

10 9 8 7 6 5 4 3 2 1

CW

Printed in the United States of America

Series design by Saho Fujii

The illustrations for this book were done in Staedtler ink on Canson Marker paper,
then digitized with Adobe Photoshop for color and shade.
The text was set in Humana Sans Light and the display type was handlettered.

CHAPTERS

CHAPTER 1

Pick a Card, Any Card

Ladies and Gentlemen, members of the press, and dog lovers everywhere…BEWARE!
I, Madame Wiley, have consulted the tarot cards, gazed into my crystal ball, read the star charts, and checked the Internet, and they all say the same thing….**He who cracks open this book shall be doomed forever!**

If you foolishly decide to proceed, I suggest you pack your silver bullets and, of course, a fresh pair of drawers. The creatures of the night await you…

We begin our story with the gruesome transformation of a man into a werewolf! Please take note of the bulging eyes, the uncontrollable drool, and the slimy, sweaty skin.

No, wait! That's just Coach Haunch, the surly,
burly coach of the Gingham County Cracklins,
the state's 100th-ranked soccer team—out of 50.

"You kids quit being rowdy on the bus!"
screamed Coach Haunch. "I've only had one
cup of coffee today and you hooligans are
working my last nerve!"

That's me, Wiley, and my best friend, Jubal, winners of the Least Valuable Player Awards for three years straight. If we look nervous, there's a good reason—our bus was on its way to Carpathian County, where we would face the most dreaded team in all of Texas—the Carpathian Coyotes!

Carpathian County was Texas's least popular vacation destination — a dreary mud puddle of a place known for its high crime rate, terrible weather, and old women with facial hair.

The Carpathian Coyotes were the state's top soccer team, and the players were famous for their monstrous abilities.

"Some folks say the Coyotes devoured the last team that challenged them," said Chucky Frewer, our team's star kicker.

FLASHLIGHT FOR SCARY EFFECT

"Others say they use a stuffed human head for a soccer ball!" said Bjorn Dasher, the team goalie.

"I hear their players aren't even human. They're made from the parts of other kids, sewn together by a mad scientist!" said Scrawny Mitchell, team marketing consultant.

"Now! Now!" said Coach Haunch. "We all know those frightening and outlandish stories are absolutely 100 percent TRUE, but that won't stop us from having a good time!"

As our bus approached Carpathian County Elementary, the sky grew dark and the terrain became treacherous. Boulders bounced off the roof of the bus.

The road was a winding nightmare. Strange howls and the smell of dead skunk filled the air.

"AAAAHHH!!!" screamed Wilky Jenson from the back of the bus. "We're being followed by a couple of wrinkled zombified freaks!"

Everyone ran to the back of the bus to take a look.

"Those aren't zombified freaks!" I yelled. "That's my Grampa and Gramma! They're coming to watch the game!"

"Look!" said Grampa, waving from his car. "The children are so happy to see us, they're screaming with delight!"

CHAPTER 2

The Drawbridges
of Carpathian County

Carpathian Elementary was about as inviting as a haunted castle full of rabid wolverines.

"Hey!" I said. "They've got a moat with real alligators!"

"I tried to get us alligators," said Coach Haunch, "but it wasn't in our budget."

Grampa and Gramma walked me to the field.

We walked up to two grave-looking women watching over a table of delicious baked goods (that is, if you think blood sausage fritters, sheep's brain pie, and crickets in a blanket are delicious).

"Oh, looky!" said Gramma. "A bake sale!"

"Beware!" said one of the pale women. "Beware the full moon! Go! Leave before it is too late! And one more thing....Please buy some of our cookies."

The Coyotes were a huge, hulking, ghoulish bunch. Coach Cretorious, the Coyotes' creepo captain, laughed at us. "Hee hee! Look at what we have here! I must warn you, my boys are hungry and they looove the taste of Cracklins!"

"Hey, coach!" said Grampa. "Looks like your team already got beat...with an ugly stick!"

Grampa's taunting angered their team mascot, Curly the Coyote, and he came over to us.

"You don't scare me, you overgrown Chihuahua," said Grampa angrily.

"Cool it!" said Gramma. "Your doctor said no more fighting with team mascots. You remember what happened with the Garland County Grackle? That bird put you in the hospital for two weeks!"

The Carpathian Coyotes' soccer field also served as a graveyard, which made sense, because we were about to get slaughtered!

We looked like wimpy little munchkins compared to those thugs.

Coach Haunch gathered us together for a pep talk before the kickoff.

"I know it looks hopeless, boys. The other team is bigger, they've never lost a game, and they've sent hundreds of boys like you to the hospital, so I've just got one bit of advice...I think it would be a good idea to fill out these Last Will and Testaments before we begin."

CHAPTER 3
Bend It Like Blech-em!

At last it was time for the kickoff, and I was the one doing the kicking. The game was afoot!

The game was a total disaster! We were kicked around.

Stomped on like grapes!

We were juggled like bowling pins in a circus freak show!

In the end, we were left in a broken heap on the field.

But the game's most shocking moment came
from the stands. The tension between Grampa
and Curly the Coyote exploded into a full-
fledged brawl.

"This mangy mutt ate my crickets in a blanket!"
yelled Grampa.

When all was said and done, we lost twenty-seven to zero, I had a minor head wound, Jubal required sixteen stitches, and Grampa suffered a nasty bite on his arm and was charged with third-degree mascot assault.

"Other than that, it was a great game!" said Coach Haunch.

CHAPTER 4

Dog Day Afternoon

Days later, we were back home in Gingham County and life returned to normal. The air was crisp, birds were chirping, all was well…

That is, until Gramma came running in and interrupted a very important science experiment on Merle, the cat.

"Wiley!" she yelled. "I'm worried about your Grampa! I think he's lost his mind, or what's left of it!"

Gramma proceeded to tell me a tale of utter madness.

"It all started the other morning when Grampa brought me the daily paper with his mouth. I guess I should have noticed that wasn't normal.

"And I didn't think anything was odd when he chased poor Merle up a telephone pole.

"Or when he slept at the foot of the bed. Frankly, it was a relief. Your Grampa snores like a congested wildebeest.

"But when he took third prize at the WestMunster Dog Show, that was just too much! I'm afraid your Grampa thinks he's a dog! And a show dog at that!"

CHAPTER 5

Canine Intervention

That night we asked Grampa about his behavior.

"Nonsense!" he said. "I'm perfectly normal. Now, if you'll excuse me—I'm going out with Esther and Chavez to chase raccoons and dig through Old Man Copperthwaite's garbage cans."

The next morning we confronted Grampa again.

"After careful analysis," I declared, "we have determined that you are suffering from Caninus Envialus, which means you wanna be a dog."

"You need help," added Gramma, "from a professional."

"Whatever you say," said Grampa, finishing his breakfast, "but I still think you guys are crazy."

CHAPTER 6

The Professional

We decided to take Grampa to a real expert on animal behavior—Nate Farkles, Gingham County's top veterinarian.

But Nate was at a loss. "I don't know what's going to be more difficult: determining why your Grampa thinks he's a dog or having to look at him in his underwear all day. This job can be pretty tough sometimes."

Nevertheless, Nate ran extensive tests on
Grampa. He took a rather large saliva sample.

Then he drew Grampa's blood.

While Grampa had a flea bath, Nate gave us his professional opinion: "I'm stumped. I'd like to run a few more tests, and I have a few more needles I'd like to stick in him. I'll have the results back to you in a few days. Until then, if he starts to act like a dog, you might just wanna smack him with a rolled-up magazine."

CHAPTER 7

Grampa, What Sharp Teeth You Have

That night, Grampa was under strict orders to get some rest and relaxation. So, while Gramma was out at her Friday night quilting session, we kicked back to watch *The All-Night Mega Monster Scare-a-thon.*

"Hi there, kiddos! I'm Claud Bones, your rotten horror host. Tonight's lineup is looking a little HAIRY! Yes, it's werewolf night! We'll start off with *I Was A Preschool Werewolf*, followed by *Honey, I Ate the Kids*, and top it off with the classic *The Mange of La Mancha*.

"Tonight's show is brought to you by Swipe, melon-scented deodorant. Remember, if you're smelling ripe, give those pits a Swipe."

"Hot dog!" shouted Grampa. "A triple feature! This calls for some triple-spicy Pork Cracklins!"

"Werewolves!" I said. "That's it! Grampa, ever since you got that bite at the soccer game, you've been acting like a canine. You might be turning into a werewolf!"

"It's a good thing there's not a full moon," said Jubal.

Suddenly, Blue Norther, channel 5's smarmy weatherman, made an announcement: "Hi, folks! Our lunar experts say there's a full moon out tonight, and you know what that means— crazies! And lots of 'em! I don't want to alarm you but, right now, your backyard could be crawling with werewolves and lunatics, probably carrying sharp objects, looking for their next victim. Have a wonderful evening!"

Just as I feared, Grampa jumped up and let out a horrendous howl.

"Boy, those Cracklins really must be spicy!" said Jubal.

"No!" I said. "Can't you see? Grampa's turning into a werewolf!"

Grampa began to transform in front of our very eyes. First, his teeth grew sharp and his eyebrows sprouted like weeds!

Then his hairy toes burst out of his shoes!

"Dude!" said Jubal. "Somebody get him some toenail clippers, quick!"

Then Grampa began to snarl, and he must have drooled at least 3 pints of saliva. (That's a full pint more than usual!)

Finally, he sprouted thick, white, disgusting ear hair. Oh wait, that's always been there.

Grampa leaped through the front window and ran off into the night.

"We've got to find Gramma and tell her about Grampa's new look!" I said. "Jubal! Merle! Quick, to the bicycles!"

CHAPTER 8

A Dog in the Fog

We hopped on our bikes and set out after Grampa, who had already left a trail of destruction. We used Merle's keen sense of smell to track the elusive half beast/half old guy.

We came upon the Gingham County dogcatcher's truck. To our surprise, the back door was open and all the lucky canine prisoners were making their escape.

"Where's Dirk, the dog catcher?" asked Jubal.

We found Dirk, shaking and babbling with fright.

"Dirk!" I said. "What's the matter, man?"

"B-b-b-biggest dog I ever seen!" stuttered Dirk. "It had white hair, bony elbows, and a terrible smell…like—like medicated ointment. I haven't met a dog that terrifying since the Great Chihuahua of Logan's Lane!"

Dirk the dogcatcher was too far gone to be of any use to us, so we headed to the Gingham Gulch Shopping Plaza.

"There's the crafts store!" I yelled. "Gramma's in there with her quilting group. Let's get her!"

"I'm waiting outside," said Jubal. "No small boy should have to enter that place!"

CHAPTER 9

League of Extraordinary Quilters

I wanted to make sure I didn't alarm Gramma too much, so I quietly snuck up behind her.

"Gramma!" I screamed, shaking her vigorously. "Grampa's turned into a werewolf and he's terrorizing the countryside!"

"Wiley!" she yelped. "Don't ever sneak up on a woman while she's sewing! I could have sewn my thumb to the table!"

"Did you say *werewolf?!*" asked Cleta Van Snout as the Ladies' Quilting League pulled out crossbows with wooden spikes.

"Actually," I said, "Grampa was bitten by a coyote in Carpathian County."

"A were-yote!" said Cleta. "Half man, and half coyote! That's even worse than a werewolf! Ten times as mean, three times as hairy."

"The only way to kill a were-yote is to shoot it full of silver-tipped wooden spikes dipped in my famous honey mustard garlic dressing!" said Martha Archer.

"How do you ladies know so much about were-wolves and were-yotes?" I asked.

"By day, we quilt. By night, we hunt werewolves," said Martha. "It supplements our incomes nicely."

"Thank you, but I think we'll find Grampa ourselves," said Gramma as we backed away from the granny werewolf killers.

We hopped into Gramma's car and set out to find Grampa. The streets of Gingham County were in total chaos!

Grampa was causing a massive panic.
"I think I know where your Grampa's headed!"
said Gramma as she stepped on the gas.

Gramma did a fancy cop-show maneuver and skidded to a halt at the foot of Grampa's favorite establishment—The Gingham County Pork Cracklin Plant.

CHAPTER 10

C.S.I.: Gingham County

Sure enough, someone had broken into the Cracklin plant. There was broken glass everywhere. We carefully opened the door.

We inspected the Cracklin plant, searching for any sign of Grampa.

Gramma dusted for coyote prints while Jubal collected fiber and whisker samples.

"Hey, look!" I shouted. "I found some muddy footprints!"

"And this looks like your Grampa's back-pain medication!" said Jubal.

Suddenly, we heard a horrible snarling sound from the next room.

"Prepare yourselves, people," I whispered nervously. "Who knows what horrors await us beyond this door."

I slowly pushed the door open to find...

Grampa was napping. The horrible snarling sound was actually more of a horrible snoring sound.

"That's your Grampa, all right!" said Gramma.

CHAPTER 11

Wanted by the Mob

Gramma wrapped Grampa in a lovely quilt and we quickly headed home. We opened the front door and found…

An angry mob of townspeople was in the living room.

"Turn him over!" they yelled. "Give us the werewolf!"

"That beast terrorized my livestock!" yelled Earl Huggins, local farmer.

"Then he went tinky on my prizewinning rose bushes!" yelled Marjorie Millner, local old person.

"Then he sang the worst version of 'Living La Vida Loca' I've ever heard!" screamed Earl Basuki, owner of the One Night in Sing Sing karaoke bar.

"Give us the old man!" shouted the mob.

Luckily, the full moon had gone back behind the clouds and Grampa had changed back to his normal bony self.

"Howdy!" said Grampa. "Boy! If I'd known everyone was coming over I would have put on some fancy cologne!"

"Look!" I said. "It's just plain ol' Grampa!"

The Ladies' Quilting League burst in and they were ready for action. "Come on, girls!" shouted Cleta. "Let's put this were-yote out of its misery! Lock and load!"

"Nooooooo!" shouted Gramma. "You can't shoot my beloved husband with honey-mustard spikes! Not over my new carpet!"

"There is one other option besides shooting
your Grampa with spikes," said Fern Thigwell,
"though it won't be as fun. There is one man in
town from Carpathian County. He knows how
to break the curse. Unfortunately, he is locked
away in a maximum security facility."

I suddenly got a bad feeling in the pit of my
stomach. I knew exactly who she was talking
about.

CHAPTER 12
Silence of the Hans

The next morning, Grampa and I went to
the Gingham County Institute for Criminal
Masterminds and Their Grandchildren
to confront an old
acquaintance.

"Vell, vell, vell!" said Hans Lotion, sitting next to his grandson, Jurgen. "Vhat brings you to my little maximum security bachelor pad?"

Hans and Jurgen had been locked away for fishnapping, assault with a deadly bass, and forty-two unpaid parking tickets.

I explained the situation to Hans and pleaded with him to tell us how to break the curse.

"I vill tell you if you promise me von zing," Hans said.

"I knew it!" said Grampa. "You won't tell us unless we help you escape this place! Shame on you!"

"Actually," said Hans, "I vanted you to bring me some extra spicy buffalo vings. Ze food in zis joint is ze pits!"

So, as Hans pigged out on hot wings, he told us how to lift the curse. "Your soccer team must defeat ze Carpathian Coyotes by ze stroke of midnight during ze next full moon. If you fail to do so, your beloved Grampapa vill be forever in ze doghouse!"

CHAPTER 13

You Gotta Be Kidding!

"Defeat the Carpathian Coyotes by the stroke of midnight?!!" yelled Coach Haunch, flabbergasted. "Boys, I don't mean to sound negative, but we couldn't beat a team of blind, one-legged chimpanzees...and believe me, we've tried!"

But I wouldn't take no for an answer. "Isn't there anything that will make you change your mind, Coach?"

"Well," he muttered, "there is one thing..."

So, as Coach Haunch pigged out on hot wings, he made an important announcement in an emergency press conference: "We, the Gingham County Cracklins, will attempt to defeat the Carpathian Coyotes by the stroke of midnight tonight in the hopes of saving this beloved, respected, and kindly old man.

"And if that doesn't work, the old ladies get to shoot him with spikes!"

CHAPTER 14

Fun with Mucus

Later I stopped by the vet to see if Nate had the test results. "Boy, do I!" Nate said. "I've managed to locate the coyote cells in this sample of your Grampa's saliva."

Sure enough, I could see the coyote cells invading Grampa's molecular makeup.

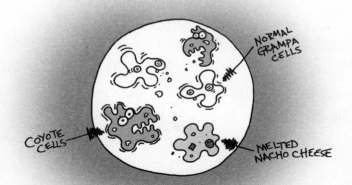

NORMAL GRAMPA CELLS

COYOTE CELLS

MELTED NACHO CHEESE

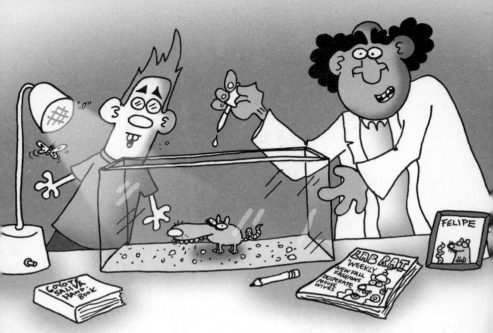

"You ain't seen nuthin' yet!" said Nate. "Just this morning I used one drop of your Grampa's saliva on my lab rat, Felipe. With a little artificial moonlight, Felipe transformed into this pint-sized were-yote! It's quite remarkable. I can't wait to try it on my mother in-law!"

Nate's dangerous experiments gave me an idea. "Nate, I'm gonna need two gallons of that coyote slobber, one hypodermic needle, and a dozen jelly donuts!"

CHAPTER 15

The Maim Event

Game night in Carpathian County! The stands
were packed with rabid soccer fans. Blue
Norther even showed up in his Whopper
Doppler Chopper.

Before the game, I gathered my teammates. "I'd like to start the game off with a new tradition. These are 'good luck' jelly donuts. Help yourselves!"

Everyone eagerly grabbed a donut.

"Wiley!" shouted Coach Haunch. "Now's not the time to be eating junk food! Besides, we just had corn dogs and milk shakes!"

CHAPTER 16

Rebooted

Just like before, the game got off to a disastrous start. We were being mercilessly mowed down by those humongous hooligans!

The Coyotes had already scored two points just ten minutes in.

"It's okay, Wiley!" yelled Grampa from the stands. "It doesn't matter if you win or lose... except that, if you lose, these old dames will slowly torture me and turn me into a human pincushion!"

CHAPTER 17
Wiley Coyote

Suddenly, the full moon burst out of the clouds!
A tingly sensation crept up my body. At first, I
thought I'd stepped in an ant mound....

But then I realized that I was transforming into
a junior league were-yote! The whole team
sprouted hair, fangs, claws, and some serious
dog breath. The crowd gasped.

Gramma and the Ladies' Quilting League were shocked at the sudden were-yote explosion.

"A whole soccer team of were-yotes!" shouted Cleta. "I sure hope we brought enough honey-mustard garlic spikes!"

"All right, I admit it!" I said. "I injected those jelly donuts with my Grampa's coyote mucus to turn us all into were-yotes! The only way we can beat these brutes is to fight monsters with monsters! If we don't beat them by midnight, we're all cursed for life!"

After the transformation, the game was a different story. We may have been smaller than the other guys, but we were fast and our teeth were sharp!

While we gnawed at the ankles of the enemy, Chucky Frewer scored our first goal of the evening…actually, it was the team's first goal in twenty years!

CHAPTER 18

Meet the Berserkers

Coach Cretorious was none too happy about our team's transformation.

"You're not the only ones with a secret weapon!" said Cretorious, approaching a giant metal cage. "Bring out the Berserkers!"

The Berserkers were the most gigantic, hideous, frightening nine-year-olds I'd ever seen. What was worse, we could see right up their nostrils.

"Jubal," I said, "there's no hope for us. We're gonna get squashed like bugs!"

Suddenly, Grampa jumped out on the field, armed with toilet paper.

"Go for it, Wiley!" he snarled. "I'll take care of these turkeys!"

Grampa used the old toilet-paper-around-the ankles trick to trip up one of the Berserkers.

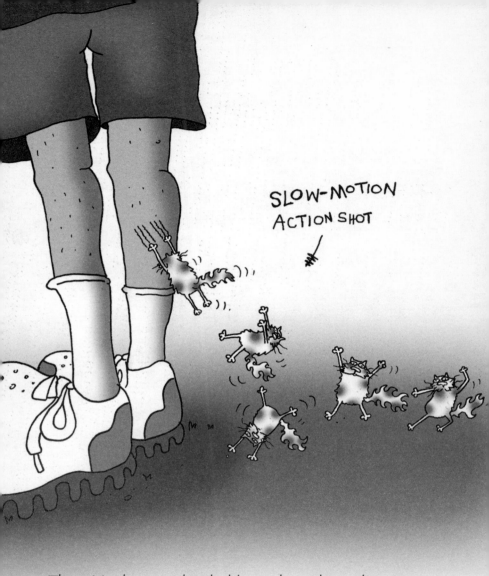

SLOW-MOTION
ACTION SHOT

Then Merle cartwheeled in and used another
Berserker's leg as a scratching post!

While Merle and Grampa distracted the Berserkers, I made a dash for the goal and nailed the shot. It was good!

"Goooooaaaaalll!" I howled. The game was all tied up!

"No fair!" whined Coach Cretorious. "This crusty, bony, hairy dog is too old to be on the field!"

"Hey!" said Grampa. "Don't hate the playa. Hate the game!"

"Boys!" yelled Gramma from the stands. "It's almost midnight! You better hurry up or you'll be were-yotes for life! Besides, I've gotta get up early tomorrow!"

That's when something terrible happened. One of the Berserkers picked up the game ball and ate it like a cheese puff!

"Oh, what a pity!" said Coach Cretorious. "That was the last of the soccer balls and now it's gone and you only have thirty seconds until midnight! Hee, hee!"

"Well, this is it, Wiley!" said Grampa, gloomily. "I guess those old women are going to get to turn us into Swiss cheese after all. "

CHAPTER 19

A Hair-Raising Development

"It's not over yet!" shouted Gramma as she stood up. Her anger meter was in the red zone. She reached up and started to fiddle with her hair.

GRAMMA'S ANGER METER

Gramma then disconnected her bun and lifted it above her head! "I have to warn you creeps," she said.

"I'm having a bad hair day!" she bellowed as she tossed me her big bun.

I took her hair and ran with it. The goal was mine. Nothing stood between me and victory now!

Actually, something horrible stood between me and victory. Curly the Coyote was the new goalie! The little beast that started this whole mess was back, looking as happy and whacko as ever!

"Move it, short stuff!" yelled Grampa as he flew in to attack Curly. "I'll show you my Peruvian Pile driver move!"

While Grampa put the smackdown on Curly, I went for the shot.

With only seconds left, I gave that bun
a swift kick.

It bounced off of Jubal's belly...

and went straight past the wrestling coyotes
into the goal! Just in the nick of time, too! The
crowd went wild and we all transformed back
into regular soccer hooligans.

CHAPTER 20

We Are the Champions

It felt good to be a boy again. The crowd showered us with confetti and roses and old food wrappers. We had won the respect of the Carpathians. Gramma put her hair back in its proper place.

Grampa stopped fighting with Curly, and the mascot even took off her mask.

"Wow, Curly!" said Grampa. "If I'd known you were just an eight-year-old girl, I never would have put the smackdown on you!"

Everything was peachy and everyone was happy…

except for the Ladies' Quilting League.

"Rats! I sure had my heart set on shooting something!" said Fern.

So that's my story.
Grampa, Jubal, and I
became soccer legends.

Gramma's removable hair was the hottest thing
for Christmas.

The Ladies' Quilting League gave up hunting werewolves and were-yotes for vampires instead.

And as for those coyote mucus-filled donuts. The last one mysteriously went missing....

And you won't believe who ate it.

The local newspaper took these two action shots for the sports section, but something looks wacky about that second picture. Help us point out the differences in these two pics before the paper hits the press!

The answers are on the next page. Anyone caught cheating gets two tablespoons of coyote saliva!